The Masterpiece

CONTENTS

For Ricker,
a fine artist and a good friend.

Chapter One

Inspiration!

The forest was filled with
the fragrance of spring. Sunlight
sparkled down on the clearing
as Fox unpacked his paintbrushes
and set up his easel.

Humming a happy tune,
Fox put a clean canvas into place.
He lined the paints up and carefully
opened each one. He placed
a bright red cap on his head.
Then he picked up his favourite
paintbrush.

"I want to paint something special," said Fox. "Something sensational, something spectacular." Fox waved his paintbrush in the air. "I want to paint a *masterpiece*!"

"What's a masterpiece?" asked Dove, landing on top of the easel.

"A masterpiece," explained Fox, pointing towards the canvas, "is the most beautiful thing you have ever seen."

"The most beautiful thing I've ever seen is the sky – clear, bright blue sky," said Dove, spreading her wings.

"Sky," nodded Fox, dipping his brush into the blue paint. "That's a good place to start."

Just then, Beaver came ambling
up from the river.

"What's going on?" she asked.

"Fox is painting a masterpiece,"
explained Dove.

"That's right," said Fox, tilting his
cap to one side. "I'm going to paint
the most beautiful thing you have
ever seen."

"Water," whistled Beaver
through her big front teeth.
"Clean, sparkling, splishing, splashing
water is the most beautiful thing
I've ever seen."

"Water," nodded Fox.
"Yes, I guess water is beautiful."

"Wait a minute!" shouted Squirrel, scampering out onto a branch. "Trees – tall, green, blow-in-the-breeze trees are the most beautiful things I've ever seen."

Chapter Two

Starring: Everyone!

Fox dipped his brush into
the green and said, "Painting
a masterpiece is hard.
There is so much to fit in."

Bee buzzed around the canvas.

"Flowers," he hummed. "Red ones,
yellow ones, purple ones, and pink
ones. Flowers are the most
beautiful things I've ever seen."

Fox was rushing from one colour to another when, suddenly, Mole popped up out of the ground.

"Dirt," he mumbled with a mouthful.

"Dirt?" cried Fox.

"Yes," nodded Mole.

"Lumpy, bumpy, gritty, grimy, good-to-dig-in dirt is the most beautiful thing I've ever seen."

Fox dipped his brush
into the brown paint.

"Mountains," growled Bear,
towering above a blackberry bush.
"Big, rocky, reach-to-the-sky
mountains are the most beautiful
things I've ever seen."

"Sky," cooed Dove.

"Water," whistled Beaver.

"Trees," shouted Squirrel.

"Flowers," buzzed Bee.

"Dirt," mumbled Mole.

"Mountains," bellowed Bear.

"All right, all right!" cried Fox, throwing his hands up into the air. "Just give me a little peace and quiet. I'll let you all know when the masterpiece is finished."

Chapter Three

The Dream

Dove, Beaver, Squirrel, Bee, Mole, and Bear all went about their day while Fox stroked lines, brushed shapes, and dabbed bright colours onto the canvas.

As the setting sun sent shadows deep into the clearing, Fox put down his brush and wearily stepped back to look at his work.

"Well," said Fox, with a yawn, "I've put in what everybody else thinks is beautiful, but..." Fox scratched his head, "there is still something missing."

Rubbing his eyes, Fox lay down under a tall tree. "Something important..." he mumbled.

Fox pulled his cap down over his eyes and fell fast asleep.

He dreamed of bright blue sky; clean, sparkling water; tall, green, blow-in-the-breeze trees; red, yellow, purple, and pink flowers; lumpy, bumpy dirt; and rocky, reach-to-the-sky mountains.

All night, the voices and faces
of his forest friends swirled around
in his head.

Chapter Four

A Little Help Goes a Long Way

A shimmering moon lifted above the treetops as Dove flew down to the canvas. Dipping her wing into the paint, she made a few quick strokes, then fluttered off again.

One by one, the other animals sneaked up to the canvas and added their artistic touch.

As the morning sun came peeping into the clearing, Fox's eyes snapped open.

"That's it!" he shouted, leaping to his feet. "Now I know what my masterpiece needs! It needs the most beautiful thing of all."

Fox ran towards the canvas and slid to a stop. His mouth fell open as he stared at the painting.

"Oh my..." he gasped. "It's, it's magnificent, but who...?"

"We did!" laughed the animals, standing behind Fox. Fox spun around to face his forest friends.

"Now your painting needs just
one more thing," cooed Dove.

"But my friends are in it already," said Fox. "What else could it possibly need?"

"YOU!" shouted the animals.

Smiling, Fox picked up the brush, painted himself into the picture, and stepped back to admire it with his friends.

"It's wonderful," whistled Beaver.

"It's spectacular," sighed Squirrel.

"It's brilliant," buzzed Bee.

"It's marvellous," murmured Mole.

"It's the most beautiful thing I've ever seen," bellowed Bear.

"Yes," beamed Fox.

"It really is a masterpiece!"

From the Author

I wrote this story in appreciation of all my good friends. Though there are many lovely things in the world, there is nothing more beautiful than friendship.

Richard Vaughan

From the Illustrator

I have loved painting and drawing ever since I was a little girl. I have worked on cartoon films and have painted pictures for exhibitions.

Jenny Press